KIRSTEN ON THE TRAIL

KIRSTEN · 1854

BY JANET SHAW

ILLUSTRATIONS RENÉE GRAEF

VIGNETTES SUSAN MCALILEY

THE AMERICAN GIRLS COLLECTION®

Published by Pleasant Company Publications
Previously published in *American Girl*® magazine
© Copyright 1999 by Pleasant Company

For information, address: Book Editor, Pleasant Company Publications,
8400 Fairway Place, P.O. Box 620998, Middleton, WI 53562.

Printed in Hong Kong.
99 00 01 02 03 04 05 06 C&C 10 9 8 7 6 5

The American Girls Collection®, Kirsten®, and Kirsten Larson®
are trademarks of Pleasant Company.

Edited by Nancy Holyoke and Michelle Jones
Designed by Tricia Doherty and Laura Moberly
Art Directed by Kathleen A. Brown, Tricia Doherty, and Laura Moberly

Library of Congress Cataloging-in-Publication Data

Shaw, Janet Beeler, 1937-
Kirsten on the trail / by Janet Shaw ;
illustrations Renée Graef ; vignettes Susan McAliley.
p. cm. — (The American girls collection)
Summary: Nine-year-old Kirsten keeps her friendship with a Sioux
Indian girl a secret until Kirsten's little brother becomes lost in the woods.
Includes a section on Sioux Indians and a project related to the story.

ISBN 1-56247-764-1
I. Graef, Renée, ill. II. Title. III. Series.
PZ7.S53423 Kig   1999   [Fic]—dc21   98-40676   CIP   AC

The
AMERICAN GIRLS
COLLECTION

™

PICTURE CREDITS

The following individuals and organizations have generously given permission to reprint illustrations contained in "Looking Back": p. 32—National Museum of Art, Washington DC/Art Resource, New York. Sioux Village, Lake Calhoun near Fort Snelling, George Catlin, 1985.66.385. National Museum of American Art, Smithsonian Institution, Washington DC; p. 33—"Indians Traveling" by John C. McRae, courtesy W. Duncan MacMillan; p. 34—Seth Eastman, *Hunting the Buffalo in Winter*, watercolor, Ayer Collection, Newberry Library, Chicago; p. 35—"Several families of Sioux Indians encamped killing buffalos, drying meat, and dressing the skins for robes" by George Catlin, from the Collection of Gilcrease Museum, Tulsa, #0176.2136; p. 37—Yankton Lakota Robe, gift of the family and friends of Natasha Congdon. 1980.352. Denver Art Museum (robe); Minnesota Historical Society (sled); p. 38—John Anderson Collection, South Dakota State Historical Society, State Archives, Pierre, Larry Sherer; National Museum of Natural History, Smithsonian (cradle board); South Dakota State Historical Society, Pierre, #1974.3.47 (moccasins); p. 39—Private Collection; p. 40—Colter Bay Indian Arts Museum, Grand Teton National Park (pouch); Collection of Glenbow, Calgary, Alberta, Canada (tool and arm cuff); p. 41—Photos courtesy of Atlatl, Inc., National Service Organization for Native American Arts; p. 42—Photography by Jamie Young.

TABLE OF CONTENTS

KIRSTEN'S FAMILY AND FRIENDS

PAPA
*Kirsten's father, who
is sometimes gruff
but always loving.*

MAMA
*Kirsten's mother, who
never loses heart.*

KIRSTEN
*A nine-year-old
who moves with her
family to a new
home on America's
frontier in 1854.*

LARS
*Kirsten's 14-year-old
brother, who is
almost a man.*

PETER
*Kirsten's mischievous
brother, who is
6 years old.*

SINGING BIRD
*Kirsten's secret Indian
friend, who calls her
"Yellow Hair."*

KIRSTEN ON
THE TRAIL

Holding her breath in excitement, Kirsten stood at the edge of the stream not far from her family's cabin. It was March in Minnesota, and the thick ice on the water had begun to melt. But Kirsten hardly noticed the sunny morning. She was looking at a little bundle wrapped in white birch bark, lying on the stones at her feet. She dropped her water bucket, knelt, and unwrapped the birch-bark packet. Inside she found a soft leather bag decorated with red and gold porcupine quills. It was almost like the one her Indian friend, Singing Bird, wore at her belt. Singing Bird was back!

Singing Bird had been one of Kirsten's first friends when the Larsons came from Sweden to make a new home in America. The two played together in the woods and often left little gifts for each other here by the stream. But many of the settlers believed that Indians could not be trusted. They felt the Indians might become angry as more farms were built on their hunting lands. Kirsten was afraid her parents wouldn't want her to be friends with an Indian, so she kept her friendship with Singing Bird a secret.

When Singing Bird's tribe moved on to search for better hunting, Kirsten thought she might never see her friend again.

As Kirsten held the leather bag, Singing Bird stepped out from the forest brush. "You're back!" Kirsten cried as she ran to her.

Singing Bird gently touched

3

Kirsten's yellow braids in greeting, as she'd always done. "Ho!" she said.

"I've missed you!" Kirsten said. "And this bag is so pretty. Thank you!" She clasped her friend's hand and squeezed hard.

Singing Bird squeezed back. With a smile she tucked the bag into the waistband of Kirsten's apron. Then Singing Bird patted her own bag. "We are sisters, Yellow Hair."

Kirsten gazed at her friend. Singing Bird was thinner than when she'd gone away. Her cheekbones were sharp and her deerskin dress hung loosely on her shoulders. "Did your tribe find good hunting?" Kirsten asked, worried.

"Do you have enough to eat now?"

Singing Bird shook her head. "We come to try our old hunting grounds again. Our tepees are not far. Come with me?"

Kirsten shook her head sadly. "I can't come now. Mama sent me to get water so she can wash our clothes. Can we meet here later?"

Singing Bird crouched and drew a sun in the sand. Then she pointed to the tops of the pines and made a sign for Kirsten to meet her when the sun reached the branches.

"Yes, I'll meet you then!" Kirsten promised.

With a wave, Singing Bird turned

and ran into the bushes. In a moment, she had disappeared from sight.

When Kirsten turned to pick up the water bucket, she saw her little brother, Peter, standing at the bend of the trail. He stared at her, his eyes wide. "What are you doing with an *Indian*?" he asked.

A flush of guilt warmed Kirsten's face. How she wished Peter hadn't seen her with Singing Bird! He might tell Mama or Papa. "You sneaked up on me!" she said accusingly as she walked toward him.

"I didn't sneak! Mama sent me to tell you to hurry," Peter said. Then he added in an excited whisper, "Who is that Indian girl? What did she give you?"

Kirsten pulled the leather bag from her waistband and stuffed it under her shawl. But she couldn't lie to Peter. He already knew too much. She put her hands on his shoulders and looked right down into his blue eyes. "Peter, do you know how to keep a secret?"

He nodded so hard his blond hair flopped down over his forehead. He loved secrets.

"Then I'm going to tell you one, but first you've got to promise never to tell anyone. Never ever!"

"I promise!" Peter said solemnly.

Kirsten took a deep breath. "That

"Peter, do you know how to keep a secret?"

Indian girl you saw with me is my secret friend."

"But Papa says we can't trust Indians!" Peter said. "He says they could be dangerous!"

"Singing Bird's not dangerous," Kirsten insisted. "She's kind and she's good—"

"And she gave you something!" Peter added.

"She gave me a bag she made. Lots of times we give each other presents." Kirsten stopped. She shouldn't have said so much.

"Presents!" Peter grinned. "I wish I had an Indian friend, too. Take me to see the Indians, Kirsten!"

But Kirsten's head hummed with worry. Surely Mama and Papa would find out if she took Peter to Singing Bird's village. They wouldn't approve, and they might even be angry. Kirsten put her fists on her hips and frowned hard at her brother. "You're much too young to meet Indians," she said in a grown-up voice like Mama's. Then she turned back to the stream, filled the water bucket, and walked quickly ahead of him toward the cabin.

Peter ran at her heels. "I'm not too young!"

"You're only six!" Kirsten hissed.

"Almost seven!" He ducked ahead of her and ran backward so she couldn't ignore him. "I'm plenty old enough to meet Indians!" As they reached the clearing by the cabin, he was still hurrying along backward, insisting, "I am not too young!"

Mama was coming from the barn with a bucket of milk. "Children!" she cried. "I won't have fighting! Stop it this minute and tell me what makes you so angry."

Kirsten ducked her head. "I'm not fighting, honestly."

But Peter folded his arms across his chest and pushed his red face near hers. "You are too fighting!" he said. To Mama he blurted, "Kirsten says I'm too young to meet her Indian friend! But her

friend's nice! She gave Kirsten a present!"
Then his face turned a darker red as
he realized he'd told the secret he'd
promised to keep.

Mama set down the milk bucket and
slowly wiped her hands on her blue
apron. "Kirsten Larson," she said in her
most serious voice, "is it true you have
an Indian friend?"

"Just a girl like me," Kirsten
murmured.

"What present did this Indian girl
give you?" Mama held out her hand.

Kirsten couldn't refuse her mother.
She took the leather bag from under her
shawl and handed it over.

Mama looked at it curiously. Then

two worry lines slanted between her eyebrows, and she tucked the bag into her apron pocket. "Look around us at the wilderness, Kirsten. Dangers are everywhere, and no one will protect us but ourselves. Papa says we don't know what to expect of the Indians these days. Your friend may be young, but we can't take the risk."

Kirsten's eyes burned with tears. "But Singing Bird just came back! She—"

"Stop!" Mama said. "You must not play with that Indian girl ever again."

Through her tears Kirsten watched Mama go into the cabin. Then Kirsten turned to Peter, who hunched his shoulders as though he wished he could disappear. "You promised not to tell!" she said in a choked voice. "Now I can't play with Singing Bird again! It's all your fault!"

"I didn't mean to tell! It just came out." Peter was crying, too, his cheeks wet and his lips trembling. "It's your fault, too! You shouldn't have had such a big secret in the first place! Anyway, I can find the Indians all by myself!" Hurt and angry, Peter ran back down the path toward the stream.

Kirsten scrubbed at her face with the hem of her apron. Disappointment and anger boiled in her chest. Her bad feelings had spilled onto Peter. But he shouldn't have told! Kirsten trudged to the cabin for breakfast.

But Peter didn't come back for breakfast. At noon, Papa and Kirsten's older brother, Lars, went into the forest to search for him.

After they'd gone, Mama paced anxiously back and forth in the little cabin. "In this spring weather, the bears are coming out of their dens to look for food after the long winter. A bear might go after Peter," she said to Kirsten. "The ice on the lakes is thawing. If he walks on thin ice, he could fall through and drown! Indians might find him and steal him. I've heard they sometimes steal little boys."

The Indians are too smart to want Peter, Kirsten thought darkly. But Mama's fears troubled Kirsten. After all, Peter was just a little boy. She shouldn't have expected him to be able to keep her secret. And she shouldn't have made her friendship with Singing Bird a secret in the first place. Surely if Mama and Papa knew Singing Bird, they would realize she could be trusted. Worst of all, Kirsten felt very guilty because it was her anger that had made Peter run away. If he got lost or hurt, it would be her fault. She wished she could help Papa and Lars look for him.

"We must keep working," Mama

finally said with a sigh. "Kirsten, please get more water for the wash."

When Kirsten reached the stream, she was startled to discover Singing Bird standing in the deep shadows under a pine tree. Then Kirsten realized that in the worry of the morning she'd forgotten this was the time they had agreed to meet here. Now she was especially glad to see her Indian friend. Singing Bird knew the forest well. She was just the one to help find Peter.

Kirsten gripped her friend's hands. "I think Peter's lost in the woods!" she said.

Singing Bird cocked her head. She didn't understand. Maybe Indians never got lost. How could Kirsten explain? She pointed to the prints her boots made in the soft mud. Then she pointed to the marks left by Peter's smaller boots.

"Peter's run off! See, he came this way. I need to follow him."

Singing Bird knelt and pointed to the hollow made by the toe of Peter's boot. "Yes, he runs," she said.

Kirsten saw that all of Peter's boot prints had the deep toe marks of a running boy. "Can you follow his tracks?" she asked.

Singing Bird smiled. "Yes. You come." She began walking quickly beside Peter's

*Singing Bird knelt and pointed to the hollow
made by the toe of Peter's boot.*

footprints. Kirsten hurried along right behind her.

When the tracks left the path and led into the woods, Singing Bird often had to crouch and look closely to find them. Where the undergrowth of the forest was thicker, she pointed to the deeper heel marks left by Peter's boots. "Here he walks," she said. Farther on, she pointed to a scrape on the moss and a handprint. "Here he falls."

Kirsten marveled that every mark meant something to Singing Bird. She could read Peter's tracks the way Kirsten was learning to read English words in a book.

They followed Peter's trail along a stony ridge and then into a ravine. Here Singing Bird pointed to tracks in the earth made by much larger boots. Papa had come this way in his search for Peter. But his tracks turned down the ravine. Peter's marks went straight up the slope. Papa had missed Peter's trail. But Singing Bird easily followed it up the hillside and into much deeper forest.

Now it was hard to see more than a little way ahead. But Singing Bird didn't hesitate. "Look," she said, showing Kirsten where Peter had broken twigs as he struggled through the thickets. When blackberry brambles stopped him, his tracks doubled back. Then, right by

Peter's boot print, Kirsten saw an animal
track she easily recognized. It was the

track of a bear!

Kirsten grasped
Singing Bird's shoulder.
"Is the bear after Peter?" she whispered.
Singing Bird shook her head.
"Hungry bear wants food, not a boy."

Though Singing Bird seemed
confident, Kirsten wasn't so sure. And
even if the bear didn't go after Peter,
a wolf might. "Let's find him quickly!"
she pleaded. Singing Bird motioned for
Kirsten to follow her again.

♥

Now two sets of Peter's boot prints

showed the way. Singing Bird drew a circle in the air. Peter was truly lost and wandering in circles. Poor Peter! *He must be frightened*, Kirsten thought. *He might even have hurt himself. Surely a wolf would attack an injured child.* Kirsten's heart beat fast with fear. Where could her little brother be?

Peter's boot prints were closer and closer together as he became tired and staggered. Singing Bird showed Kirsten where he'd stumbled over a fallen branch. Then, at the bottom of a hill, Singing Bird stopped, took Kirsten's arm, and pointed.

At first, all Kirsten saw was a fallen log. But when Singing Bird led her closer,

she saw Peter sound asleep inside it! His face was smeared with dirt and tears, his shirt was torn and muddy, but he didn't look hurt. Singing Bird gently touched his shoulder.

Peter opened his eyes. At the sight of Singing Bird, his mouth opened in alarm.

Quickly Kirsten knelt by him. "It's

24

us, Peter! Don't be scared! You were lost, but now you're not lost anymore!"

"You're sure I'm not?" Peter asked in a small voice. He was still staring at Singing Bird.

"No, you're not lost," Kirsten assured him. "Singing Bird found you. And now she'll show us the way back home. Come on, get up."

When they reached the edge of the woods near the cabin, Kirsten gave Peter a push. "Run on ahead and show Mama you're safe," she told him. "She's worried sick!"

Peter scampered as fast as a squirrel

around the end of the fence and toward the cabin.

Singing Bird stopped and drew back. "I go now," she said seriously.

But Kirsten wanted Mama to meet Singing Bird and understand that she was the one who had found Peter. Surely then the hurt caused by the secret would be healed, and Kirsten could play with her friend again. She took Singing Bird's hand. "Please come to our cabin," Kirsten said. "Come meet my mother."

Still, Singing Bird hung back and shook her head. She looked frightened.

Now Kirsten remembered how strange the Indian village had seemed to her the first time Singing Bird took her there. Maybe Singing Bird's parents had warned her not to go near the settlers' cabins. Maybe she had never met a settler woman before. "It will be all right," Kirsten said firmly, hoping it would be. Clutching Singing Bird's hand tightly, Kirsten led her to the cabin.

Inside, Mama was hugging Peter and scolding him at the same time. When she saw Singing Bird, she pulled Peter closer to her. "Kirsten, is this the Indian girl I told you not to play with?" Mama asked.

"This is Singing Bird," Kirsten said. "And she's my friend. But we weren't playing. Singing Bird tracked Peter through the woods. She saved him, Mama!"

Mama looked doubtful. "Is this true?" she asked Peter.

"I went looking for Indians, but one found me instead," Peter said.

Now Mama's face softened. "Then I thank you for your help," she said to Singing Bird.

"Can I have something to eat now?" Peter asked. "Can I have bread and honey?"

"Of course!" Mama said. "And you must eat with us, Singing Bird. You are welcome here." Smiling, Mama slipped the little leather bag from her apron pocket and handed it to Kirsten.

Kirsten tucked the leather bag back into the waistband of her apron.

"Wouldn't you like some bread and honey?" she asked her friend. When Singing Bird nodded shyly, Kirsten said, "Then come have some with us!"

JANET SHAW

Doug and me

Now

When I was a kid, I had braces on my teeth and often Band-Aids on my knees. My brother Doug and I explored the woods by our house and played in Hinkson Creek, which ran through the woods. We built a hideout of branches on a sandbar in the middle of the creek. We named the place Sand Island. When I was sad or upset about something, I went alone to Sand Island to think things through.

Janet Shaw is the author of the Kirsten books in The American Girls Collection.

LOOKING
BACK
1854

A PEEK INTO THE PAST

THE SIOUX IN 1854

When white settlers began entering Minnesota, two major Indian groups lived there, the Sioux and the Ojibwa.

A Sioux village near Fort Snelling, Minnesota

Singing Bird's people were the Sioux. She belonged to a band that lived in Minnesota and called themselves the *Dakota*. Dakota means friends or allies. *Sioux* is similar to the Ojibwa word for "snake."

In the 1840s and 1850s, large numbers of settlers moved into Minnesota and beyond. By 1854, the Ojibwa and Sioux had *ceded* (SEED-ed), or given up, most of their land in Minnesota to the United States. White settlers had overrun Indian hunting grounds and killed many animals that the Sioux depended on for food. The wild animals were also leaving the land because the settlers were building farms. The Sioux didn't have enough to eat, so they were forced to leave to find enough food.

The Sioux were nomads. They took their tepees apart and moved them each season to find food. In the winter the Sioux set up tepees in the shelter of trees, and men hunted on snowshoes. In the early spring they moved their camps to sugar maple groves for several weeks to make sugar. The men hunted ducks,

In the winter, the Sioux hunted on snowshoes.

geese, and other animals. In the late spring they returned to their permanent summer bark lodges to plant crops like corn, pumpkins, and beans. They also gathered roots and berries. During the summer, some groups traveled with tepees to hunt buffalo. In the fall, women collected wild rice, and men went on a big fall hunt. When the men returned, the women preserved the meat and other food for the winter.

The Sioux women in front of the tepees are scraping a buffalo hide to use as a tepee covering.

Many settlers on the frontier were afraid of Indians because they did not know or understand them. Some pioneers made friends with Indians. Others believed Indians were blood-thirsty savages. Kirsten didn't know what to believe until she met Singing Bird, an Indian girl.

Indians often helped the settlers by sharing food and shelter with them. Pioneers traded guns and tools for furs and buckskins from the Indians. Pioneers also learned about corn planting from Indians. They taught the pioneers to save the best kernels from their harvest and soak them in water and herbs. This helped them grow faster when they were planted the following year. Without help from the Indians, many settlers would not have survived.

Until whites came, everything the Sioux had or used they made themselves. When they killed a buffalo, they used each part. They ate the meat, made the hair into rope, and dried the stomach to use as a cooking vessel. Indian women used

Native Americans like the Sioux and the nearby Hidatsas made robes and sleds from buffalo hides and bones.

the skin to make tepees and clothing.

Indian women did all the cooking and made all the clothing. Indian girls helped the women cook, carry water, and gather wood. They also learned to sew their own clothes, pouches, and moccasins.

Women and girls used beads and

Sioux women dyed porcupine quills to embroider the leather on cradle boards and moccasins.

porcupine quills to decorate clothing and many other things like jewelry, tools, and toys. Quillwork took a lot of patience—and a lot of quills. A quilled purse like Singing Bird's could take four days to make and might have as many as 140 quills!

An Ojibwa pouch decorated with quills

One of the hardest parts of quill-work was collecting the quills. This was done by Indian men. They didn't want to kill porcupines just for their quills. And luckily they didn't have to. Porcupines move very slowly, so a man could throw a blanket over a porcupine and then set the animal free. The quills stuck to the blanket, and the man could pick them out.

Women and girls did the quillwork. First, they sorted and dyed the quills, and then they softened them by sucking on them or soaking them in water. Finally, the quills were flattened and sewn or woven onto bark or animal hides.

Quills were kept in pouches and flattened with an iron tool.

Some quillwork designs were shaped like triangles or squares. Others looked like flowers or animals.

The quills on this arm cuff are sewn in the shape of a star.

Quillworkers also got design ideas from their dreams. These designs were considered holy.

Today, many Sioux Indians live on reservations in North and South Dakota or in cities across the United States. They are proud of their past and carry on many Sioux traditions. Some Indian women still teach their daughters to quill and bead in the hope of keeping these traditional arts alive.

Modern Sioux art

MAKE A CHARM BAG

Charm a friend with a pretty bag.

Kirsten knew that Singing Bird was back when she found her leather pouch near the stream. When Singing Bird appeared, she tucked the pouch into Kirsten's apron. The gift showed how much Kirsten meant to her. Make this charm bag for your special friend or to store your own treasures.

You Will Need:

♥ *An adult to help you*

Chamois, 4 1/2 by 11 inches*

Scissors

Leather spring punch*

Needle

Waxed thread*

Scraps of felt, optional

Glue

Hole punch

Leather thong, 45 inches long

* Available at leather supply stores. To find a leather store, look under "Leather" or "Leather Supplies" in the yellow pages of the phone book.

Chamois (SHAM-ee) can also be found in the automotive section of department stores.

1. Fold the piece of chamois in half lengthwise. Round off the top edges of the chamois.

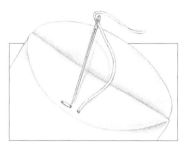

2. Fold one rounded edge down. Use the spring punch to make three holes through the flap and the first layer of the chamois. Sew down the flap.

3. Glue scraps of felt to your bag in a pretty design.

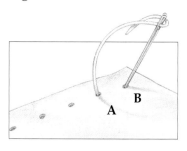

4. To close up the sides of the bag, use the spring punch to punch holes 1/4 inch from the edge and 1/4 inch apart along the sides of the bag. Then sew a backstitch through the holes. To backstitch, come up at A and go down at B.

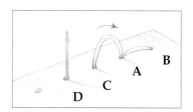

5. Come up at C. Then go down at A and come up at D. Tie a knot close to your last stitch, and cut off the extra thread.

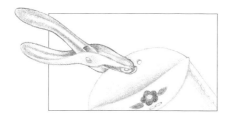

6. To make your bag into a necklace, use the hole punch to make two holes at the top of the bag.

7. Thread both thong ends through the holes. Pull them back up through the thong loop to make a knot. Tie the ends around your neck.

THE AMERICAN GIRLS COLLECTION®

To learn more about The American Girls Collection, fill out the postcard below and mail it to American Girl, or call **1-800-845-0005**. We'll send you a free catalogue full of books, dolls, dresses, and other delights for girls.

I'm an American girl who loves to get mail. Please send me a catalogue of The American Girls Collection:

My name is _____

My address is _____

City _____ State _____ Zip _____

My birth date is ____/____/____   1961
                  Month   Day   Year

And send a catalogue to my friend:

My friend's name is _____

Address _____

City _____ State _____ Zip _____

                                              1225